The Boxcar Children Mysteries

MYSTERY IN THE CAVE

created by
GERTRUDE CHANDLER WARNER

Illustrated by Charles Tang

SCHOLASTIC INC.
New York Toronto London Auckland Sydney

ISBN 0-590-56898-1

Copyright © 1996 by Albert Whitman & Company. All rights reserved. Published by Scholastic Inc. by arrangement with Albert Whitman & Company. THE BOXCAR CHILDREN is a registered trademark of Albert Whitman & Company.

12 11 10 9 8 7 6 5 4   6 7 8 9/9 0 1/0

Printed in the U.S.A.   40

First Scholastic printing, January 1996

Contents

CHAPTER 1

Alone in the Dragon's Mouth

The Alden family loved boats —
houseboats, rowboats, ferry boats, and sail-
boats. But they had never been in a boat that
went through a cave before.

Now they were floating along a stream under the earth!

"Aunt Jane was right," James Alden said
to his four grandchildren. "She's told me
many times that we shouldn't miss the Dragon's Mouth Cavern and this tour with her
old friend, Nelly Stoner. I have to agree."

"Me too," fourteen-year-old Henry said,

leaning back to enjoy the ride. "And you know what else? Now we won't have to hear Benny beg to visit here every time Aunt Jane mentions it. We finally made it."

"Finally," Benny agreed. "Good thing you found us living in our boxcar in the woods, Grandfather. Now that you have a big family, you get to take big family trips."

Mr. Alden grinned at his six-year-old grandson. "That's certainly true. It's much more fun to visit places with the four of you."

"And a lot more exciting," Henry said.

"Quite true," Mr. Alden agreed. "You children always seem to get into some kind of adventure."

"But we haven't had any kind of adventure on this trip," Benny complained.

Violet Alden, who was ten, pulled her sweater sleeves over her chilly hands. "Hunting for rocks and crystals for the next few days will be plenty of adventure for me."

The tour boat, with its many passengers, rounded a curve and glided under a limestone bridge. The Aldens sat back to listen to Nelly Stoner.

"Now we're right under the natural bridge we walked over at the beginning of the tour," the cheerful older woman said to the passengers. "Doesn't it look just like a man-made bridge?"

"It sure does," Benny said. He twisted his head this way and that. He wanted to get a good look at the amazing stone bridge. "How did this bridge get made, anyway?"

Nelly Stoner chuckled. "Our young passenger here just asked how this bridge was made," she said loudly so everyone on her tour could hear. "Can anyone tell us?"

When no one spoke up, Benny's twelve-year-old sister, Jessie, raised her hand. Mrs. Stoner nodded to Jessie.

"There was probably a very small hole in the limestone millions of years ago," Jessie began. "Then water started pushing through it and made the hole bigger and bigger until it was an arch. At least that's what my book about caves says."

"That's exactly right," Nelly Stoner said as she steered the boat to a small dock. "This brings us to the end of our tour. Please stay in your seats until the boat comes to a full stop. We'll meet by the elevator. Then I'll bring everyone up to the Cavern Gift Shop."

When the Aldens and the other passengers were out of the boat, Mrs. Stoner looked around and flashed a light toward the back of the cavern. "That's funny. I was sure there were twenty-two people on this tour. Now I count only twenty."

The passengers checked around to see if anyone was missing, but no one could tell.

Mrs. Stoner turned to Mr. Alden. "Perhaps I miscounted, James. If you don't mind, I'll bring everyone else up on the elevator. Then I'll return for you and your grandchildren. Now don't go getting lost down here."

"Don't worry about that, Nelly," Mr. Alden answered.

"Goody," Benny said after the elevator doors closed. "Now we can be down here by ourselves. Maybe we'll have an adventure after all. These lights could go out and we could get stuck down here."

Jessie held up a flashlight. "Not to worry.

Henry and I brought along two of these, just in case. Not that we'd need flashlights. Mrs. Stoner said the Dragon's Mouth Cavern has had electricity ever since it opened to visitors a *long* time ago."

"I like visiting this cavern, but it's just a tour with lights and music and a boat," Henry said. "I'd like to do some *real* caving, where you crawl through skinny, dark spaces, and you don't always know where you're going."

"You children may well find some real caves while you're out rock hunting over the next few days," Mr. Alden said. "Nelly Stoner says that many nearby caves connect to this one."

Benny still couldn't get over all the strange forms in this underground world. "I'm sure glad we can't see that dragon shape we saw on the tour from here. The spotlight made its eyes glow when we went by it on the boat."

Violet and Benny took each other's hands. It was awfully quiet now that the other visitors were gone.

"I didn't like the dragon shape either," Violet said. "Too scary."

Suddenly, everyone jumped.

"Did you see shadows move over there?" Benny whispered, squeezing Violet's hand.

Mr. Alden walked ahead a few steps. "I thought perhaps all these lights were playing tricks on my eyes."

The Aldens jumped again a minute later when the elevator door opened.

"Whew. Glad it's you, Nelly," Mr. Alden said. "We thought somebody else might be down here."

Nelly Stoner looked puzzled, too. "You know, something odd may be going on. I thought I had two more people on this tour, but I'm not sure which two. We've had so many visitors today, one face started to look like another. I went back to the ticket booth to count the stubs for this tour. There were twenty-two, but only twenty people came off the boat. I'll take you up to the gift shop and then come back to check around."

"Can we check, too?" Benny begged.

"We're good at finding missing things, especially if they're people."

Mrs. Stoner gave Benny a friendly pat on his head. "Now, now. We won't need that. Just go have fun in the gift shop. I know from your Aunt Jane that you collect rocks and crystals. Our shop is full of wonderful things. Enjoy yourselves. I'll join you later."

With that, the Aldens stepped into the oversized elevator. When the doors reopened, the Aldens found themselves in a large gift shop. Its shelves were filled with souvenirs, rocks, crystals, and fossils.

"Have a good time," Grandfather said. "I'll drive over to the Dragon's Mouth Motor Court to reserve a cabin. By the time you finish shopping, I'll have you all checked in. See you in half an hour or so."

The children hardly knew where to look first. Benny headed to the glass shelves crammed with fantastic purple, green, and gray crystals.

Violet picked up a small polished stone with the tiny skeleton of a snail in it. "I'd

like to buy one of these snail fossils."

"What I need are batteries for my head-lamp," Henry said to Jessie. "I haven't used it since my caving trip last year. If we do find a cave, I want to make sure we have plenty of fresh batteries for my lamp and our flashlights."

Jessie nodded. "I'll get a couple small candles, too. I read someplace that cavers should always have two kinds of lights."

"Good thinking." Henry turned to Violet. "We'll meet you and Benny by the elevator."

For the next half hour, Benny and Violet walked slowly up and down the aisles. After browsing for a while, they went over to the elevator to wait for Henry and Jessie. That's when they noticed the elevator panel light up.

Violet said, "Mrs. Stoner must be bringing the elevator up again."

The next thing Benny knew, he heard the whoosh of the doors and felt someone bump hard into him. "Whoa!" he said, trying to keep his balance.

Violet steadied her brother. "You okay? Those two people raced out of there without looking."

Benny tried to catch his breath. "Was Mrs. Stoner one of the people?"

Before Violet could answer, Nelly Stoner was right there. "I hope you children had a good time in the shop. Maybe you can come down to the cavern with me, after all."

Benny's mouth opened wide. "But — but," he sputtered. "Didn't you just get off the elevator?"

"I've been meeting with my staff the way we do every day after the final tour. We've been counting ticket stubs and money for the last twenty minutes. I came up a few minutes ago," Mrs. Stoner said. "I didn't see any sign of those missing tourists."

Violet's blue eyes grew wide. "Two people just got off the elevator. Maybe they work here."

Mrs. Stoner shook her head. "That can't be. The staff's all been with me. Maybe those were the two people who got lost. I suppose we'll never know."

Benny pointed to the elevator panel. "But we saw the numbers light up. Then somebody almost made me fall."

"Now tell me, what did these people look like?" asked Mrs. Stoner.

Violet and Benny didn't answer right away.

Finally Violet spoke up. "We didn't get a good look. Everything happened so fast. We just saw two blurs go by."

Violet and Benny were still talking when Jessie and Henry returned.

"Hi, you two," Henry said, wearing his headlamp. "How do I look? Want to try it on, Benny?"

But Benny and Violet weren't paying any attention to Henry's headlamp. They had their hands cupped against the shop window so they could see out to the parking lot.

"They got away," Benny said in a disappointed voice.

"Who got away?" Jessie asked. "What's going on?"

Nelly Stoner tried to explain. "We're

trying to figure out who rushed off the elevator."

"Maybe it was the two people who got lost on the tour," Jessie said.

Mrs. Stoner nodded. "That could be. But this is the first time any visitors came up by themselves. I suppose I shouldn't worry about it. Oh, here comes your grandfather."

"Sorry I took so long, everyone. I nearly had an accident," Mr. Alden explained. "Just as I was pulling out of the motor court to get back here, a motorist raced into the exit instead of the entrance. Good thing I pulled to the side, or we would have hit each other."

"Did you see the driver?" Mrs. Stoner asked.

"No," Mr. Alden answered. "The car was green, but it went by so fast I didn't see much more than that."

"Are you all right, Grandfather?" Jessie asked.

"I'm fine," Mr. Alden said. "Anyway, I reserved the cabin. The manager told me there are some excellent crystal formations nearby where you can collect all the rocks you want. What do you think of that?"

"I think I'm ready to go rock hunting," Benny said with a smile.

CHAPTER 2

The Sky Is Falling

The Aldens spotted the Dragon's Mouth Motor Court right away. A huge green dragon was outlined in lights from the top of its head to the tip of its tail. Instead of breathing fire and smoke, this dragon flashed the words: COZY CABINS HERE.

"How are we going to sleep with that big flashing sign?" Benny asked.

Mr. Alden laughed. "Don't worry about that. The owner, Mr. Howe, gave you a cabin in back. Wait until you see it."

Mr. Alden drove through the motor court.

Small cabins encircled a swimming pool and playground. "Our cabin is up on Little Nose Cliff. Someone wanted to rent it, but Nelly Stoner made sure Mr. Howe set it aside for us."

Mr. Alden pulled up next to an old green car in the parking lot at the bottom of the cliff. In a flash, Benny was out of the station wagon and up the steps leading to the cabin. At the top, he shouted down to everyone. "Hey! This cabin is built right into the rock!"

After the long climb up, Violet joined Benny. "We'll be just like a bear family living in a cozy den," she said when she looked around.

Benny ran to the back room where two beds were set against a stone wall. "Neat! I never slept inside a rock before."

Jessie put down her suitcase. "You and Henry take this room. Violet and I will sleep on the fold-out couch in the front room."

"I knew you children would find this cabin very snug," Grandfather said. "You know I have to be away to do some business for the next few days. Mrs. Stoner and Mr. Howe will be right in the motor court if you need anything. She said she'll keep an eye on you."

Henry carried his suitcase and Benny's into the bedroom. "We won't need a thing, Grandfather. There's a stove, a refrigerator, and a sink, too."

Violet hugged her grandfather. "I'm glad we're staying here and not in a fancy hotel. It's like being in our own house."

"This is almost as much fun as our box-car," Benny said.

After Mr. Alden left, Jessie unpacked the picnic basket and the cooler the family brought on all their car trips.

"Mmm," Benny said, watching every bit of food Jessie put away in the refrigerator. "What's for supper tonight?"

"Looks like ham and eggs," Henry said, helping Jessie. "And I'll make some fried potatoes, too."

Soon everyone was busy cracking eggs, peeling potatoes, and cutting up the leftover dinner ham Mrs. McGregor, their house-keeper, had sent from home.

"Let's eat out on the little porch," Violet suggested. "There are four chairs and a table out there."

Though it was dark outside, the Aldens didn't mind eating outdoors at all. Jessie found a length of string and tied one end to a hook on the porch ceiling and the other end to her flashlight. "There. Now we have an overhead lamp. I'll light one of the candles I bought and put it in the middle of the table. That way we can see our food."

"Nothing is nicer than eating outside," Violet said when she sat down. "This reminds me of living in our boxcar."

"Only now we get to sleep on real beds instead of straw," Henry said.

After supper, the sounds of singing crickets outside and clinking silverware inside filled the air. The children dried the dishes together. It had been a long day. They were ready for bed.

Benny had opened his mouth to yawn when something — a noisy, rumbling *something* — hit the porch roof.

"What's that?" Henry yelled over the rat-

tling sound. He ran to the front door but didn't open it. "It sounds like rocks falling on the roof. Let's stay inside so we don't get knocked on the head."

Jessie put her arms around Benny and Violet. The children stared out the front window as small rocks tumbled down. No one moved. Finally the noises stopped.

Henry slowly opened the door and the children tiptoed out to the porch. "Maybe there was an animal climbing overhead," he said, trying to see in the dark, "and that sent a bunch of rocks down."

Everything was quiet now except for the sound of a very loud motor down below in the parking lot.

"Look, there's a car driving away," Jessie said to Henry. "Do you suppose there were rock climbers on this cliff?"

Henry shook his head. "Pretty foolish ones if they were out at this hour. Rock climbing is dangerous enough in daylight, let alone at night. Let's tell Mr. Howe what happened."

When the Aldens went to the registration desk, they found Mr. Howe snoring in his easy chair. His reading glasses were still perched on his nose, but his newspaper had fallen to the floor.

"Mr. Howe, Mr. Howe," Henry called.

Mr. Howe kept right on snoring.

Violet read a small sign on the counter. "It says 'Ring bell for service.' "

When he heard the bell, Mr. Howe's blue eyes flew open so fast that his reading glasses fell off his nose. He shook himself awake, then brushed back the few strands of hair on his head.

"Can I help you, folks?" he said. "Need a cabin?"

Jessie stepped up to the desk. "Our grandfather rented us a nice cabin, Mr. Howe. He said to see you if we needed anything."

Mr. Howe stared at the Aldens. It took him a while to figure out who these children were. "Of course, of course. Your grandfather told me you'd be arriving. Hope you like Little Nose Cabin. I usually don't rent it out to families. Don't want children getting hurt up on Little Nose Cliff or throwing rocks down. But Nelly Stoner told me you all were careful."

Jessie wished she didn't have to tell Mr. Howe about the falling rocks. "Um, we just — um — we just came down to tell you — uh . . ."

". . . how much we like our cabin," Henry said, stepping up to the counter. "Thanks for letting us have it. We just wanted to say hi." With that, Henry signaled the others to go outside.

"But I thought we were going to tell Mr. Howe about the falling rocks," Jessie said on the way back to the cabin.

"We were," Henry whispered. "Then he mentioned he doesn't usually rent the cabin to families. I don't want him to think we were throwing rocks or anything. Let's see if we can figure out by ourselves what happened."

"It's too dark to do anything tonight. Let's go to sleep," Jessie said, leading the way back with her flashlight. "Tomorrow is our rock hunting day."

"These steps feel as if they got steeper

while we were gone," Benny said in a tired voice. "I wish this cabin had an elevator."

"Whew. Finally," Henry said when they opened the front door.

"Hey!" Benny yelled, suddenly a lot more awake. "How did my suitcase get out here? I put it away in the closet."

"I put mine there, too," Violet said, spying her blue duffel bag in the middle of the room.

Henry opened all the drawers of the bedroom dresser. Then he checked his suitcase, which was also in the middle of the bedroom. "That's strange. Nothing's missing — not money, not our camera. Hey, wait! Where's my headlamp? I'm pretty sure I left it right on the dresser."

The children checked the whole cabin. Henry's headlamp was nowhere to be found.

Henry shrugged. "As far as I can tell, somebody moved all our luggage from the closet. Unless I left my headlamp in Grandfather's car, I think somebody took it. The question is, *why* would anybody want it?"

"I don't know," Jessie said, "but I'm double locking this door right now."

Everyone decided it was too late to figure anything out tonight and got ready for bed. Benny crawled under his covers and said to Henry, "I'm sleeping with my suitcase right under this bed." But before Henry could say anything, Benny had drifted off to sleep.

CHAPTER 3

An Underground Monster

By eight o'clock the next morning, nearly every table in the Dragon's Mouth Coffee Shop was filled. The Aldens stowed their backpacks and rock hunting tools under the last empty table. They could hardly wait for breakfast.

Mr. Howe soon arrived to take their orders. " 'Morning, Aldens. I recommend the flapjacks. The cook happens to be a good friend of mine — been married to her for forty years. Meantime, let me fill you up with orange juice."

"We're going rock hunting today, and I'm going to find a Rockville 'diamond,' " Benny announced. "See, here's a picture of one in my rock book."

Mr. Howe took a look at Benny's book. "Hmm. I've got a Rockville 'diamond' on display right behind the cash register. You can go get it, young fella."

Benny dashed off and returned a few seconds later with a crystal-clear rock chunk. It looked amazingly like a huge diamond.

"You should lock this up," Benny said with excitement. "What if it's a real diamond, not just a crystal? It could be worth zillions of dollars."

"Then I'd be a zillionaire and have to retire to a golf course. That wouldn't be nearly as much fun as running my motor court and coffee shop, would it?"

"Nope, I guess not," Benny answered. He turned the clear rock crystal every which way to catch the light. "Look, Jessie. It's like the one in my book."

"It sure is," Jessie agreed. "Now we'll know what to look for."

While they waited for their flapjacks, the Aldens passed around the Rockville diamond before Benny put it back.

"Those flapjacks will last you awhile," Mr. Howe said later when the Aldens came over to pay the check. "Now let me get a look at your rock hunting gear. I can lend you some of my own tools, if you'd like. Rock collecting's one of my hobbies when I'm not here or at the registration desk."

Henry opened up a canvas duffel bag. "We have a real geologist's hammer, plus some chisels, a guidebook to the best areas, some gloves, brushes, and a strainer."

Mr. Howe checked the Aldens' equipment carefully. "Good. I see some safety goggles in here, too. Don't forget to put them on when you're hammering rock. You don't want a rock splinter in your eye. As for this guidebook, you won't be needing that. I'll let you folks in on a secret. Hike all the way to the top of Little Nose Cliff then down the other side. Some interesting rocks at the bottom were uncovered when it was blasted to make room for a road over there. I just bought a hundred acres on that side, so it's okay by me if you chisel there. If you hammer long enough, you might find some of our Rockville diamonds buried in the rock."

"Hey, thanks, Mr. Howe," Henry said.

The Aldens were nearly out the door when Mr. Howe gave them one last piece of advice. "There's a big meadow at the bottom of the cliff. Good place to have lunch. Just watch out for any sinkholes in the ground. I haven't had a chance to really explore any of the sinkholes since I bought the property. But some of them go down into caves. So watch where you step. Don't worry though, there are so many ways out of the caves it is almost impossible to get lost."

"Good thing I packed our lights and candles," Jessie said on the walk back to Little Nose Cliff. "We'll be ready in case we do find a cave. I just wish we had Henry's headlamp."

Henry sighed. "Me too. Maybe a hiker thought the cabin was open for anybody and took the headlamp. Since nothing else is missing, I didn't want to worry Mr. Howe about it in case it's in Grandfather's car. Well, I'm not going to let it spoil our rock hunting. Let's have a good time."

Forgetting Henry's headlamp, the Boxcar Children made their way up Little Nose Cliff past their cabin. Up and up they went, careful to watch every step so they wouldn't slip or send rocks tumbling down.

"Look at this view!" Henry said when everyone got to the top.

Violet looked down at the motor court far below. "The cabins and cars seem like dollhouses and toy cars from way up here." They headed down the other side.

"Neat rocks," Jessie said when the children got to the bottom of the cliff. "The colors and surfaces are different on this side of the cliff." She dug into the duffel bag for Benny's rock book and flipped the pages until she found what she was looking for. "I think this is the kind of rock that's supposed to have the Rockville diamonds in it."

Benny touched the rock. "I don't see any diamonds. Just plain old rock!"

Henry put on a pair of goggles and handed

another pair to Benny. "They don't just fall in your lap, Benny. We have to dig for them inside the rock."

The children took turns sharing the goggles and the hammer. They chipped and chipped at different sections of rock. Two hours later, they still hadn't found anything that looked like the famous Rockville diamonds.

After a while, Jessie noticed that Benny wasn't having much fun. "I know it seems as if we just ate breakfast, but it's almost lunchtime. I'm hungry from our long hike. How about you, Benny?"

Benny took off his safety goggles and licked his lips. "I'm hungry for our ham sandwiches. And something cold to drink, too. All this hammering makes me thirsty."

Everyone collected their equipment and searched for a picnic spot away from the road.

"Let's try the meadow Mr. Howe mentioned," Jessie said. "We can come back to this rock later."

"This meadow is pretty, but I wish we could put our blanket down in some shade," Violet said. "How about by that tree and some bushes over there?"

Violet led everyone to a cool spot near some rocks and a shady tree. Jessie and Henry spread out the blanket. Then they laid out the food and poured ice-cold lemonade into their cups.

Benny gulped his lemonade and sandwich, then put down the cracked pink cup he brought everywhere with him. "That tasted good," he said, ready to explore again. "Hey, guess what? There's cool air coming from this hole in the ground — whoops — "

"Benny!" Violet cried out.

The other three children ran over to where Benny had been standing. He was gone!

"Benny! Benny!" Henry yelled. "Where are you?"

"Down here, *here*, *here*," the children heard Benny's voice echo from somewhere below. "Fell in, *fell in*, *fell in*."

"It's a sinkhole into a cave!" Henry said

when he looked down. "Benny's right here. Jessie, run back and get our flashlights and some rope."

"I'm okay, *okay*, *okay*," Benny said, not sounding a bit worried. "It's just a little ways down."

"Hang on, Benny," Henry yelled into the hole. "Here we come."

When Jessie came back with the rope and flashlights, she sat at the edge of the sinkhole, then lowered herself down with no problem. Benny was there, holding his penlight to see better.

"Isn't it neat down here?" Benny asked, grinning. "Wait till you see the rest."

"Shh, here comes Violet." Jessie stood to the side so Violet would have plenty of space to climb down.

"I'm glad you're safe, Benny," Violet said. "I was afraid this hole went way way down, and we'd never find you again."

"Well, here I am," Benny said, just as if he were standing in Grandfather's back-yard.

Since Henry was so tall, he came down

with no trouble at all. Then he turned on his flashlight to get a better look at the cave.

"It slopes down then turns into a long tunnel," Jessie said, going a bit ahead of the others. "I wonder if anyone knows about this cave."

"I think so!" Benny cried out. "Look! There are footprints in the dirt. See?"

The children beamed all their lights to where Benny was pointing. Indeed, deep footprints led down toward the end of the cave.

Benny was really excited now. "Can I go ahead a little bit, Jessie? Can I? Please?"

Jessie gave a nod. "Okay, but just a few feet," she said. "First let me tie this rope around your waist. We don't want you to disappear again."

The others beamed their lights so Benny could see where he was going, which wasn't too far. He sounded brave, but he didn't want to disappear either. Staying within the light beams, Benny took a few steps down the tunnel. He was just a few feet in front of Jessie when he suddenly ran back and nearly slipped on the muddy floor.

"A monster!" Benny yelled. "There's a monster in this cave!" His voice was shaking now. "I saw giant footprints and something like a big tail print right behind them. It must be the dragon!"

"Let me look," Jessie said. Beaming her flashlight on the muddy floor, Jessie saw what Benny had reported: huge footprints, followed by a pointed, flat track. Something awfully big — maybe a giant tail — had been dragging on the ground!

With each step, Jessie took a deep breath. There *had* to be an explanation.

"Did you see the monster tracks?" Benny asked when Jessie returned.

Jessie swallowed hard before she answered. "I saw tracks, but they could be anything."

"Anything with a lot of feet and one big tail!" Benny said.

"Come on, let's talk about this outside," Henry suggested.

The children went back to the sinkhole entrance. But before they could climb out of the cave, two giant feet came through the sinkhole.

"What?" Jessie said in a hoarse whisper.

The feet were followed by legs, then the whole body of a man who was even taller than Henry.

"Who's down here?" a man's voice boomed as he pulled a large burlap sack down behind him.

The Boxcar Children nearly froze to the cave floor.

Henry stepped forward to greet the man. "Hello, we're the Aldens. We're exploring down here."

The man flashed his own flashlight to get a better look at the children. "Who?"

"The Aldens," Jessie said in a firm voice. "We were rock hunting nearby on Mr. Howe's property. He told us we could. Then we found this cave by accident and decided to look around. What's your name?"

The man didn't answer. He turned away from the Aldens and headed to the sinkhole entrance.

Benny was right behind. "I'm Benny Alden. Do you have your lunch inside that big bag? We have a bag, too, but it's on our picnic blanket. Were you going to have your lunch down here because it's so hot outside?"

The man snorted but didn't answer Benny's question.

"I guess I'll call you Joe Caveman," Benny said.

Whether he liked this name or not, Joe Caveman wasn't about to become friends with the Aldens. He whirled around, heaved his bag up, then boosted himself up from the sinkhole.

"Why was Joe Caveman in such a hurry to get out of here when he saw us?" Violet asked.

"I don't know," Henry answered.

"And I wanted to ask him if he's ever seen the monster," Benny sighed.

"Maybe *he's* our monster," Jessie said.

CHAPTER 4

A Mysterious Visitor

The next day, the Aldens didn't want to waste a minute. They were going back to the "monster" cave. They had a quick breakfast of cold cereal and milk instead of going to Dragon's Mouth Coffee Shop.

"Today we wear our oldest jeans and tops," Jessie told her brothers and sister. "And boots. It's muddy in that cave. You never know when you might come across an underground stream."

"Or even a lake," Henry said. "Let's see. I think I've got everything — ropes, flash-

37

lights, candles, a roll of reflective tape, and a first-aid kit, too. It's a perfect caving day — no rain in the weather forecast, so we won't have to worry about flooding."

Jessie helped Violet and Benny zip up their backpacks. "While Henry and I finish packing, you two run down to Mr. Howe. Tell him where we're going and when we'll be back. Careful cavers always do that before they set out."

"Do careful cavers always bring food along, too?" Benny asked.

"Of course," Jessie said, "so don't worry about that."

By the time Violet and Benny reached the coffee shop, it was nearly empty. Mr. Howe was at the register ringing up Nelly Stoner's bill.

"Jessie said to tell you we're going caving," Benny announced.

Mrs. Stoner smiled at the two children. "Are you now? And what cave are you going to?"

Violet looked up at Mrs. Stoner. "A cave that — "

"Has a monster in it!" Benny cried out before Violet could answer. "A monster with big feet and a tail and everything. I found a sinkhole to a cave. It has monster tracks in it."

Mrs. Stoner's eyebrows shot up. "Whoa, slow down, Benny. You don't mean the dragon monster? Why, that's only the name of one of the shapes in the big cavern. We do have a few live critters in our caves, but they're small — salamanders, bats, and such. Occasionally some other animals wander in."

"A man wandered into the cave we were in," Violet explained. "But he wouldn't tell us his name."

"I called him Joe Caveman," Benny said. "He wouldn't tell us what was in his big sack, either."

Mr. Howe scratched his chin. "Hmm. Could be any number of local spelunkers."

"Lunkers?" Benny asked. "What are those?"

"I'm a spelunker," Mrs. Stoner said. "And so is Mr. Howe and a lot of other folks around here. Spelunkers are people who explore caves. That's their hobby. I bet your Joe Caveman is a spelunker. His sack was probably full of caving supplies."

"But what about the monster tracks?" Violet asked. "Henry and Jessie saw them, too."

Mr. Howe shook his head, smiling. "Well, you children will just have to become spelunkers and find out all about that monster. I'll want a full report. In the meantime, I have an important job for you when you visit your cave."

"What is it?" Benny asked in an excited voice. "We like important jobs."

Mr. Howe leaned on the counter. "Here's what you do. Get a stick a few feet long and tie a handkerchief at the top. Then poke it in the ground right by the sinkhole entrance before you go down again."

"I know why!" Violet cried. "If we're gone too long, someone can find us. But don't worry, Mr. Howe. Henry and Jessie won't let us get lost."

"I'm sure they won't," Mrs. Stoner said as she left the coffee shop with the children. "I know you Aldens will have fun. The caves around here don't go too far, so you'll be just fine. Besides, I know from your Aunt Jane that you children know how to take care of yourselves no matter where you go. Good luck."

The Aldens had plenty of good luck. After coming down Little Nose Cliff they spotted the sinkhole with no trouble at all. This time Benny didn't fall in.

"There!" Benny said when they reached the entrance. He poked a long stick in the ground.

Violet tied a purple bandana to Benny's marker. "It looks just like a flag in case anyone wants to find us."

Henry held up a roll of silver tape. "We won't be needing a rescue with this. We're going to stick pieces of this reflective tape on the walls as we go in. Then we'll follow them when we come out. It's simple."

"You forgot something," Benny said before Henry could say anything else.

"What's that?" Henry asked.

"Good cavers always bring plenty of food and water," Benny answered.

Henry handed everyone their backpacks. "Good thinking, Benny. Ready? Put your hats on now so we don't get drips in our eyes."

One by one, the Aldens threw their packs down the sinkhole then lowered themselves into the cave. Today, the four heavy-duty flashlights they carried made it easy to see that the cave stretched out quite a ways.

The Aldens were careful. At every turn, Henry put up a small piece of tape to mark the place.

Benny aimed his flashlight at the cave floor. "There are those monster tracks again! Can we follow them, Jessie?"

Jessie turned around. "Not just yet. Since this is our first time in this cave, we'd better not go off on a wild goose chase."

"I wonder if we'll see Joe Caveman today," Benny said after the children began walking.

Violet shivered. "I wish we would see some other cavers. It's so quiet down here.

There could be a storm outside or even a truck driving over where we're standing, but we wouldn't know it."

Step by step, Jessie led the group deeper into the cave. Suddenly she stopped so fast, Benny bumped smack into her. "Wait!" she whispered. "I hear a clinking sound. And there's a speck of light up ahead, too."

Henry squeezed by to get a look. "Shh. Let's turn off our flashlights for a minute."

Except for the light in the distance, the cave was pitch-black. The children felt their way along the walls with their hands. Everyone took small steps so they wouldn't slip or bump into each other. Finally, they got close enough to see where the bright light was coming from.

Benny tapped Jessie on the shoulder. "Is it Joe Caveman?"

"No, it's a woman," Jessie whispered. "She's wearing a hard hat. She just put down something. Should we say anything, Henry? I don't want to scare her."

"Let's turn our flashlights back on so she can see us," Henry suggested.

"Hello? Hello?" Jessie called out. "Coming through."

Blinded by the flashlights, the blond young woman couldn't see the Aldens very well. "Who's there?" she yelled. Before getting an answer, the Aldens saw her put away a camera and some other equipment in a duffel bag. Then the woman turned off all but one spotlight.

Jessie walked ahead of the others. "We're the Aldens. We're caving down here. How about you?"

The woman zipped up the bag and shoved it back with her foot. She stared a long time at the Aldens before answering. "I'm — uh — Crystal Hollowell. I just discovered this cave while I was out hiking and decided to come in. I'm a — a — biologist — at the Rockville Community College. I wanted to see what kind of animal life there is down here."

Benny looked up at the woman. "Did you fall down the hole, too?"

Crystal didn't bother to answer Benny's question. In fact, she looked upset to see the

Aldens there at all. "Children shouldn't be allowed down here by themselves. Caves are delicate environments. They get damaged easily. I advise you to stay away from these caves."

"Our family is friends with Nelly Stoner, who runs the Dragon's Mouth Cavern. She told us all about caves and rocks and how to be careful around them. And I've done some caving myself," Henry reassured her.

The young woman's jaw tightened. "You didn't tell this Mrs. Stoner person about this cave, did you?"

"Sure we did. And Mr. Howe, too," Benny piped up. "Henry and Jessie said you always have to tell somebody when you're going caving. Did you do that?"

"I most certainly did not," Miss Hollowell answered back. "Otherwise people who don't know anything would be down here ruining everything."

Jessie tried to figure out why Miss Hollowell seemed so annoyed. "I thought you found this cave by accident," Jessie said, staring at the duffel bag. "You brought tools and lights."

Miss Hollowell nudged her bag even farther back. "These aren't tools, young lady. As for the lights, well — uh — I bring them with me whenever I go hiking just in case I have to go into dark places to study — uh — animal tracks and so forth."

Benny whirled around and pointed down the cave. "Did you see the giant monster tracks back there? We did yesterday and today."

This annoyed Miss Hollowell even more. "You were in here yesterday, snooping around? Was anyone else with you?"

"Nope," Benny answered. "But we met Joe Caveman."

"Joe Caveman?" Miss Hollowell said. "Someone else was down here? Who was it? Was he alone?"

The children looked at one another. Why did this woman mind that other people liked to visit this cave too?

"Benny made up the name when the man

wouldn't tell us who he was," Henry explained. "He was the only person we saw."

"Did he have anything with him? Tools and such?" the young woman demanded.

Jessie shrugged. "He had a big bag. That's all we saw."

Crystal Hollowell gathered up her belongings.

"I wish we had spotlights like that," Benny said. "Or a headlamp. Henry had one, almost like yours, but it disappeared. I bet we could find the monster if we had lots more lights."

"What nonsense. This equipment is for scientists, not children," Miss Hollowell told the Aldens.

"Did you find any animals?" Violet asked.

Miss Hollowell looked puzzled. "Animals? What animals? Now, can you please make room so I can get by? All of you should leave, too. There's supposed to be a big rainstorm today. This cave could get flooded." With that, Miss Hollowell disappeared down the cave without even saying good-bye.

The Aldens decided to leave, too. They turned back, this time with Henry in the lead. "Boy, Crystal Hollowell sure thinks she owns this cave, don't you think, Jessie?"

Jessie didn't answer Henry's question. She hadn't moved a step yet except to shine her flashlight on the cave wall that Crystal Hollowell had just been standing near. "Take a look at this wall," Jessie said.

The others came over to see what Jessie was talking about.

"It looks as if someone chipped away at it," Henry said. "There are stone chunks all over the floor. And she was the one who said people shouldn't come down here and ruin things."

Jessie ran her fingers over the stone. "It seems odd for someone who studies plants and animals to be hammering cave walls."

"Let's ask Mrs. Stoner or Mr. Howe about Crystal Hollowell," Henry suggested. "If she teaches at the local college, they probably know who she is."

" 'Specially if she's one of those 'lunkers," Benny said. "Like we are."

The other three children laughed as they made their way back to the entrance.

"Okay, you two," Henry said to Benny and Violet. "I've got a game. I stuck eleven pieces of tape on the walls when we came in. I want Benny to find each piece with his flashlight, and Violet can peel them off. We have to take everything out that we brought in just the way we do on our hikes."

Finally the Aldens reached the circle of sunlight shining down on the cave floor.

"Hey, that's another thing," Henry said, when he saw the sunlight. "Miss Hollowell said we should get out of the cave because a rainstorm's coming. But there isn't a cloud out today. She doesn't want anybody down in this cave, that's for sure."

Henry cradled his hands to give the younger children a boost up. One by one, they popped up from the sinkhole. Everyone was glad to get out and stretch in the warm sun after their chilly underground visit.

"Hey, look what I found," Benny said when they started toward the cliff. "A shovel."

Jessie looked at the shiny red shovel. "It

looks new. Maybe Crystal Hollowell dropped it on her way out."

"Or maybe somebody else was here but left when they saw our stick and flag," Benny said.

"That could be," Jessie said. "People seem to want this cave to themselves. I wonder why?"

CHAPTER 5

The Aldens Get a Warning

When the Aldens got back to their cabin, they put away their caving equipment and backpacks.

Henry put the red shovel in a closet. "At suppertime I'll call Rockville Community College from the coffee shop. Maybe Crystal Hollowell knows about this shovel."

Jessie pulled out some beach towels and suntan lotion. "How about a swim between now and supper?"

"Yippee!" Benny cried.

The Aldens trooped down to the pool and immediately jumped in.

"See, Henry, I can do a dive now," Violet called out from the diving board. She put her feet together, gave a bounce, and went into the water straight as an arrow.

"Nice dive!" Henry yelled back.

"Watch me, Henry!" Benny cried from the shallow end of the pool. He swam all the way across before bobbing up like a porpoise.

Violet swam over to the shallow end, then boosted herself up to get warm. "I liked caving, but it's fun being out in the sun now. I hope we can come back early every day so we can swim."

The Aldens were so busy talking and swimming, they didn't notice that two men on the side of the pool were listening to every word.

"We'll try to get back early for a swim tomorrow," Henry told Violet. "But don't forget. We promised Benny we'd follow those monster tracks. We may be down in the cave a long time tomorrow."

One of the men, a tall man with dark hair and a moustache, stepped into the pool. He began swimming laps right next to the Aldens. When the children stopped swimming, the man did, too. "I'm Randall Pitt," he said when he came up for air. "Did I hear you kids talking about caves around here?"

Henry stopped swimming. "Hello. I'm Henry Alden, and that's Benny, Jessie, and Violet. We were talking about some caving we did yesterday and today. Are you a spelunker, too?"

"A what?" Mr. Pitt asked.

"You know," Henry said. "Someone who goes caving for fun."

The man looked confused for a second. "Sure, I guess you could say that. That's my friend Ed Lyme over there. We've been caving before, only not around here. No way."

Henry looked surprised. "Why not around here? This is one of the best caving areas in the country. Every guidebook says so."

"It's none of my business," Mr. Pitt began, "but you should know something the guidebooks don't tell you. Caving's not kids' stuff — not around here anyway."

When Jessie heard this, she had to speak up. "What do you mean? We've read a lot about caving. We followed all the safety rules and came out just fine."

"Then you were lucky," the man said, turning to Jessie. "Your guidebook probably didn't tell you about the cave-in that happened a couple years back. Bunch of kids down there nearly got crushed when part of the cave came down on their heads. Just a friendly warning, that's all," the man said before he left the pool.

The children felt goosebumps up and down their arms, but not from the cold water.

Violet could hardly get her words out. "A cave-in? Why didn't Mr. Howe or Mrs. Stoner tell us?"

Henry watched the two men hurry from the pool area. "Good point. They'd never let us go into the local caves if there'd ever been a problem. Look, it's nearly time for supper.

Let's dry off and head over to the coffee shop."

For once, the word "supper" didn't make Benny jump up and down. Now he was shivery and a little sad, too. Until Mr. Pitt showed up, Benny couldn't wait to go on a monster hunt in the cave. But not if it might come tumbling down on his head!

"Don't worry, you two," Henry said when he saw Benny and Violet lagging behind. "I bet Mr. Pitt doesn't know what he's talking about."

"Hey, why such long faces?" Mr. Howe asked when he greeted the Aldens. "I saw you folks splashing in the pool having a good time. Anything wrong?"

Henry spoke up first. "One of the guests here, a Mr. Pitt, told us there was a cave-in around here a couple years ago."

"He said some kids were almost crushed," Violet whispered.

"I don't want to go to any more caves that might fall down on us," Benny added.

Mr. Howe leaned over to hear the children better. "What cave-in? Our local caves are safe as can be. Never had anyone lost, or hurt, or anything. I'd be the first to know if there was a cave-in. And I certainly wouldn't tell my guests to explore them if there'd *ever* been any trouble."

"Do you know Mr. Pitt?" Jessie asked. "He's got dark hair and a moustache and a friend, Mr. Lyme, with not too much hair and no moustache. I think they were on the cavern tour the other day."

"I know who you mean. Checked in here the night you did. Kept pestering me for your Little Nose Cabin. Raced out of here when I told 'em it was already taken. But then they came back again and took another cabin. Can't say I like those pushy types."

"Me neither!" Benny announced. "Now I don't feel like caving anymore."

Mr. Howe led the children to a booth. "Look, here's Nelly Stoner. I promise she'll tell you the same thing I said. There's never been a cave-in around these parts."

Mrs. Stoner was happy to see the Aldens. "What cave-in are you talking about? We have plenty of caves nearby but certainly no cave-ins. The only exciting thing that ever happened in our caves took place about ten years ago. The police caught a bank robber hiding down there. I believe the man's been in jail ever since. But a cave-in? Never!"

"You're sure?" Jessie asked. "One of the guests told us to stay away from any caves around here."

Benny pulled at Jessie's sleeve. "And know what? A lady we saw in the cave said so, too."

Mrs. Stoner patted Benny's hand. "Oh, it's probably some local person who wants to keep everyone else out, particularly young people. She probably didn't know how careful you Aldens are when you go hiking and caving. Not many other children could be trusted down there without an adult. Did you catch the woman's name?"

"Crystal Hollowell," Henry answered. "Do you know her? She's a biologist at Rockville Community College. We were going to call her in a little while. We think she left a shovel behind by mistake."

Mrs. Stoner was puzzled by this information. "The name sounds a bit familiar, but I don't think it's from the college. I teach a geology course there. As far as I know, no one by that name is on the staff. A biologist, you said?"

Jessie nodded. "The thing is, Miss Hollowell didn't seem to know much about animals or plants or anything that ties into biology."

"And know what else?" Benny cried. "She said it was going to rain, but it was sunny out. She said we better get out of there. And — and . . ." Benny took a deep breath. "And she said she found the cave by accident. But she had a big bag of caving stuff with her."

"We found her down there by accident," Jessie continued. "She had all sorts of spotlights and equipment. When she saw us in the cave, she stuffed everything into a duffel bag so we couldn't see it."

Henry slid out of the booth. "I'm going to call the college right now. I want to find out if Crystal Hollowell works there or not. She might have left a brand-new shovel right on

the ground. Order me whatever you're getting, okay, Jessie?"

Mr. Howe came over to take everyone's
orders. "I hope you straightened out these
children, Nelly. I wouldn't want them to
miss out on our wonderful caves just because
of someone telling tall tales. I can't say I was
too fond of Mr. Pitt and Mr. Lyme. I had
to tell 'em several times to slow down when
they're driving in the motor court. Now,
what'll you folks have?"

Everyone ordered spaghetti, Benny's fa-
vorite dish. In a short time, Mr. Howe came
by and set down five dinners, including
Henry's. "Where's your brother?" Mr.
Howe asked Violet.

"He had to make a phone call to find out
about a woman we met in the cave," Violet
answered. "Her name is Crystal Hollowell.
Do you know her, Mr. Howe?"

"Can't say that I do," he answered before
going back to the kitchen.

Mrs. Stoner put down her fork without
taking a bite. "Crystal Hollowell. Suddenly

that name rings a bell. What did she look like, Jessie?"

"About your height, blue eyes, I think, but I'm not sure. Even with all our flashlights, it was hard to tell," Jessie explained. "She also had frizzy blond hair tucked under her hard hat."

Benny leaned across the booth. "Know what? She had on a headlamp almost like Henry's! Only his was stolen from our cabin."

"You had something stolen from your cabin?" Mrs. Stoner exclaimed. "Did you tell Mr. Howe?"

"Not yet," Jessie said. "We were so tired when we unpacked our things the first night. Henry wondered if he dropped it or left it in Grandfather's car."

"Guess what?" Henry said when he came back to the booth. "There's no Crystal Hollowell at Rockville Community College. Not in the biology department or in the local phone book either."

"I was just trying to remember if I've ever

met her," Mrs. Stoner said. "It sounds so familiar to me, but I can't quite place it. I am sorry to hear that your headlamp is missing, Henry."

"Me too," Henry said. "I know I had it in the souvenir shop when I got new batteries for it. And I think I left it on the dresser in the cabin. But it was so late, maybe I didn't." Henry lowered his voice. "I didn't tell Mr. Howe yet. I don't want him to think I'm careless. Anyway, nothing else is missing."

Mrs. Stoner put down her fork. "Actually, I have something missing. A rubber raft my staff uses in the Dragon's Mouth Cavern has disappeared. We keep it tied by the wooden steps where the tour boat pulls in. But it's been gone for a couple days. I suppose it may have floated away, but I wonder . . ."

"Maybe we can find it," Benny said, his eyes sparkling. "We're going to look for the monster, and maybe we'll find a stream or an underground lake! Unless somebody chases us out again."

"I certainly hope not," Mrs. Stoner said. "Now I'm off. I want to check my address book for that woman's name, or I won't be able to sleep a wink tonight."

Suddenly Benny tapped Mrs. Stoner's arm. "Wait! She's over there. That's her talking on the phone — Crystal Hollowell."

Mrs. Stoner and the other Aldens looked up. They saw Miss Hollowell cup her hand over the phone. Benny strolled over to a gumball machine next to the pay phone. Miss Hollowell lowered her voice. Benny dropped in a nickel. Out came a gumball. Benny took his time before coming back to the booth.

"I heard what she said!" Benny whispered when he returned. "She told someone she's going to be famous if somebody doesn't get in the way. She's meeting the person she was talking to in fifteen minutes."

Mrs. Stoner and the Aldens weren't in any rush to leave the coffee shop now. Not until they spoke to Miss Hollowell, anyway.

The Aldens caught her on her way out the door.

"Miss Hollowell, Miss Hollowell!" Henry called out. "Wait up. We found your shovel near the cave."

When she heard this, Miss Hollowell whirled around. "My shovel? What shovel? What did it look like?"

"It's a red metal shovel for digging dirt," Henry said.

Miss Hollowell put her hands on her hips. "That — uh — it could — uh — be mine. Where exactly did you find it?"

"Right outside the sinkhole," Jessie said. "We can show it to you. It's up in our cabin."

Crystal Hollowell checked her watch. "I can't go right now. I have to meet someone."

Henry opened the door for the woman. "If you're going caving tomorrow, you can meet us at the sinkhole entrance. We'll be there around ten o'clock. We'll bring the shovel with us."

"Make sure you do!" Miss Hollowell said in a sharp voice. "An expensive piece of equipment like that doesn't belong in the hands of a bunch of children."

"We'll have it, don't worry," Henry said. "We wouldn't keep something that belongs to someone else. Oh, have you met our friend, Mrs. Stoner? She thinks she might know you. Nelly Stoner, this is Crystal Hollowell."

Mrs. Stoner put out her hand, but Miss Hollowell went out the door without shaking hands.

Mrs. Stoner and the Aldens watched the young woman back out her pickup truck, then race from the parking lot with her tires squealing.

"Have you met her before?" Jessie asked.

"Definitely not," Mrs. Stoner said. "I certainly would recall meeting a rude young woman like that, but I never have. I must be thinking of someone with a similar name."

"I wonder who it is," Violet said.

CHAPTER 6

Danger! Keep Out!

The next day, the Aldens had another clear day for hiking and caving. On top of Little Nose Cliff, a soft, warm breeze was blowing, and the children stopped to enjoy the view.

Benny pointed his binoculars down below. "Hey, I see Miss Hollowell down at the sinkhole entrance. She's standing next to her truck."

Henry borrowed the binoculars and took a look, too. "You're right, Benny. That is Miss Hollowell. She keeps walking back and forth and looking up. Let's all wave at the same time so she knows we're on our way down."

The Aldens began waving wildly.

"I'm not sure she sees us," Jessie said. "We'd better get down there before she leaves."

"I haven't got all day," Miss Hollowell said when the Aldens joined her down below. "Do you have that shovel you told me about?"

"Sure do. Here it is," Henry said.

Miss Hollowell grabbed it quickly, then just as quickly dropped it. "That's nothing but an ordinary dirt shovel," she said to Henry. "I can't believe I came all the way over here to look at that."

"Sorry," Henry said. "I thought you heard me say yesterday it was only a dirt shovel. It must belong to someone else."

"Probably one of the many people you told about this cave," Miss Hollowell said. "Well, if you do find the owner, here's my phone number. I'd like to know who else is using this cave."

Henry stared at her. "I tried to call you at the college. They said there was no one by your name working there."

Miss Hollowell didn't answer right away. "That's because I'm not teaching this term. I — uh — I only taught one course there — a night course. I don't live in the area, so I'm not listed in the phone book, either. Anyway it's nobody's business where I work."

"We just wanted to return the shovel, that's all," Jessie explained.

Miss Hollowell stomped with her muddy boots on the ground, climbed into her truck, and drove off without another word.

"At least we won't run into her today," Violet said.

"I wonder if she just came out of the cave," Jessie said. "Her boots were covered with wet mud, but it's not muddy out here. I'd like to take another look at that spot where we saw her yesterday. If she went there this morning, maybe we'll find something."

The Aldens threw their backpacks down the sinkhole along with the mystery shovel, then slipped into the cave one by one.

"Let's leave the shovel here," Henry suggested as he cut up pieces of reflective tape. "It's too heavy to carry very far, and we don't need it. Now! Where to, everybody?"

Jessie had a plan. "First let's go to where we saw Crystal Hollowell yesterday and see if we find anything strange there. I still say she wasn't down here studying animals. After that we'll come back and follow Benny's monster tracks."

Since they had already visited the cave twice, the Aldens moved quickly through its twisting tunnels. Each time they made a turn, Henry marked the spot with silver tape.

"Look, here's that place that's a little confusing," Henry said when the tunnel branched off in several directions. "Let's pile some of these small rocks on the floor. We'll use them as markers so we don't take the wrong turn when we come back."

The children arranged several rocks by the turn, then marked the spot with a big piece of tape.

"Good, now we can go," Jessie said. "The place where we met Crystal Hollowell should be just a little farther."

But very soon, the Aldens couldn't go another inch. Blocking the tunnel was a large rock. On it, in big white letters, were the words: DANGER! KEEP OUT!

"Hey, this wasn't here yesterday!" Benny touched the painted letters with his fingers. "And know what else? This paint is still wet!"

Henry shone his flashlight up and down the rock. "Somebody went to a lot of trouble to move this here. I don't think one person could do it alone."

Jessie knelt down with her own flashlight to get a better look. "Look, two sets of footprints. Some made with flat boots and the others with heeled boots. Did anybody notice which kind Crystal Hollowell had on?"

The other children shook their heads.

"All I noticed was the wet mud on her boots," Violet said.

"I don't see how she could have moved a

boulder this big by herself, but I didn't see anybody else in her truck, either," Henry said.

"I guess we'd better turn back. This rock is way too big to move without special equipment," Jessie said. "Let's check out those monster tracks of Benny's instead."

The Aldens couldn't stop talking about the big rock. Who had moved it? And why? What was the danger sign all about? The four children were so busy discussing the rock, they forgot to check their silver tape markers.

"Wait! Everybody, stop!" Henry said when he realized their mistake. "We forgot to follow the markers."

All together, the Aldens flashed their lights up and down the walls, looking for the reflective tape.

Nothing.

"Wait here," Henry said to the younger children. "I'm going to go back. While we were talking, we must have passed our tape markers and those rocks we put down. I bet we took a wrong turn."

"Be careful, Henry," Jessie said. "Here,

tie the end of this rope to your flashlight. I'll
hold onto the other end. That way we won't
get separated."

"Good thinking," Henry said before he
disappeared into the darkness.

"Henry won't get lost, will he?" Violet
asked Jessie.

"Not as long as he has this rope," Jessie
answered. She stared at the coil of rope unwinding as Henry went deeper into the cave.

"It's dark in here without Henry's light,"
Benny whispered.

Jessie put down her flashlight and dug
around in her backpack. "Look, Benny, I'll
light one of these candles I brought along for
emergencies."

Benny's brown eyes looked like shiny
lumps of coal in the dim light. "Is this an
emergency?"

"Not really," Jessie said, but her voice
didn't sound as sure as her words.

Then she looked down at the rope coil. "I
guess Henry is coming back. The rope isn't
unwinding anymore. Henry! Henry!" she
called out.

For some time the children heard nothing but water drops dripping, one by one, from the cave ceiling onto the floor.

"Why doesn't Henry answer?" Violet asked. "He wasn't going very far."

Jessie cleared her throat so she wouldn't sound nervous. "I'm going to tug on this rope and pull Henry in, just like a great big fish!"

Benny tried to laugh at Jessie's joke, but no sound came out. Pulling slowly, Jessie expected to feel the rope tug. But it didn't. Instead, she wound up yards and yards of loose rope. But there was no Henry at the end of it!

"Oh, no!" the children said when they saw the dangling rope.

Jessie held it up. Even in the dim light she could see that the end was smooth, as if it had been cut with scissors or a knife.

"Maybe the rope snapped on a sharp rock," Jessie said. "I've got an idea on how we can find Henry."

"What?" Violet asked.

"Well," Jessie said, "we have three flash-lights and some candles. We'll walk in the same direction Henry went. At the first place the tunnel branches off, I'll light a candle and leave it there. Then I'll light another one a little closer. Henry will see the candlelight and find his way back to us!"

This sounded like a good plan. The children joined hands with Jessie in the lead. They went down the tunnel as far as the first turn. Jessie lit a candle, then moved on ten feet and lit another one.

"Henry!" Jessie called out. "We're over here!"

"Henry!" a voice repeated back.

But it was only an echo of Jessie's voice. Jessie didn't call out for Henry again. The echo made the cave seem so empty.

"Come on," Jessie said at last. "We'll just wait for Henry right here. I know he'll find us. Mr. Howe said no one is ever lost for very long because there are so many ways out of the cave. Now let's have some lunch to pass the time."

Eating lunch did pass the time, though none of the children seemed to really taste the food. Henry still didn't come back.

"All we can do is wait," Jessie said. "You two can turn off your flashlights. We'll just leave mine on." Jessie knew they would need to save their batteries if they were down there much longer.

"The drips from the ceiling sound like the ticks of a clock," Violet said after a while. "Only it's such a slow clock."

Jessie checked her watch. An hour had passed since Henry disappeared, but in the dark, cold cave, the time seemed much longer.

Suddenly Benny nudged Jessie in the ribs. "I hear footsteps coming from the other way."

"Me, too," Violet said. "And look, there's a light. But it can't be Henry, because that's not the way he went."

"Jessie! Violet! Benny!" a deep voice called out.

"Jessie! Violet! Benny!" an echo repeated back.

"It's Henry!" Benny shouted. "Hooray!"

Jessie raced over and gave Henry a huge hug. "Thank goodness it's you! How did you get over here? We left two candles down the other way so you could find us."

"Whew!" Henry said, throwing down his hat and taking a drink from his water bottle. "I searched high and low for our markers, but I couldn't find any of them — no tape, no rocks, no footprints even. It's as if *something* made them disappear."

"Or someone," Jessie said in a low voice. "Anyway, how did you find us?"

"Well, the rope snapped. On a rock I guess. I didn't notice right away and thought it was still connected to your end. By the time I figured out that the rope *had* snapped, I was lost."

"Were you afraid, Henry?" Benny asked, holding his breath for an answer.

"Not really," Henry said, "but lucky for me all these caves connect. I found an exit out of the cave, all the way over by the Dragon's Mouth Cavern. Then I ran back to the sinkhole entrance we came in and started our first route all over again."

"How will we get out if the tape is gone?" Violet asked. "We could get lost again."

Henry held up the roll of tape. "Not to worry. I just stuck on some more pieces as I came in, right up to this spot."

"Can we go outside now?" Benny asked. "I'm cold, and I want to finish my lunch where I can see what I'm eating!"

"Me, too," Jessie said.

Just as Henry said, getting out was easy. Soon, the children spotted the daylight coming through the sinkhole entrance. They helped each other out, then plopped down on the grass.

"We sure had a scare, didn't we, Henry?" Benny asked, now that everyone was safe and sound. Then his eyes opened even wider than usual. "Hey, look! Joe Caveman is climbing out of the sinkhole!"

Sure enough, when the Aldens looked up, Joe Caveman was pulling his sack up from underground.

Benny ran over to him. "We got lost today and had to eat our lunch down there. Did that ever happen to you?"

Joe Caveman didn't seem to hear Benny. He went right on putting things into his sack.

When everything was packed up except for a book, he tied the top of the sack and threw it over his shoulder.

"Were you the one who took down our silver tape and moved our rocks?" Benny asked.

Joe Caveman didn't answer.

Jessie held up the red shovel. "Is this yours, by any chance? We found it nearby."

Without answering, Joe Caveman just politely tipped the brim of his hat, walked right by everyone, then disappeared down the road.

The Aldens looked at each other.

"What a strange man," Jessie said. "He tipped his hat, but he didn't even stop to talk. I wonder what's in that old sack of his, anyway."

"I don't know," Henry answered. "But did you see the title of the book he was holding?"

"What did it say?" Violet asked.

"*Treasure*," Jessie said.

CHAPTER 7

Benny Meets the Monster

That evening the Aldens decided to make a homemade dinner in their cabin. They made a delicious stew, and served it with hot rolls and salad. After dinner, they played cards out on the porch.

After a while, Violet put down her last card. "Want to play another round, Benny?"

"No, I want to *eat* another round. I wish we had some dessert after our dinner."

Jessie put her finger to her lips. "Shhh. You're making me hungry again. How about a nice apple, Benny?"

"Only if it's in a nice apple pie!"

Jessie laughed. "I give in, Benny. Let's go down to the coffee shop for apple pie. There's no point staying in a motel if we can't go out for dessert once in a while. It's getting chilly out, so bring a jacket."

The Aldens bundled up, then headed down the steps of Little Nose Cliff. When they reached the bottom, they noticed an empty, beat-up, green car parked under the streetlamp.

"That's the car that was here the night we arrived," Henry said. "I wonder why it's parked way over here? Our cabin's the only one at this end of the motor court."

The children walked down the road. They had nearly reached the coffee shop when they heard a car coming up fast behind them.

"Move over!" Jessie said to Benny and Violet before turning around. "That car is going awfully fast."

The Aldens jumped to the side just in time to see the green car whiz by.

"Hey, how do you like that?" Jessie asked. "It's the green car from the parking lot. I wonder if that's what almost hit Grandfather's car our first night here."

Benny tapped Jessie's arm. "And what about that car we saw the first night when the rocks fell on our cabin? Maybe it was this car."

"Right," Henry said. "The engine sounded the same. Very loud."

When the children reached the coffee shop, Henry opened the door for the others to go in first. "Let's ask Mr. Howe about that green car. He'll know."

"Howdy, Aldens," Mr. Howe said when he saw the children. "I hope you're in the mood for apple pie. I made an extra today."

"Good thing," Benny said. "Apple pie is what we came for."

Mr. Howe returned shortly with five glasses of milk and a big slice of pie to go with each one. "Hope you don't mind if I join you. I like some pie and a glass of cold milk before I go on duty at the registration desk."

Henry didn't even look at his pie. He had to find out about that fast green car. "Do any of your guests have a green car?"

Mr. Howe finished a bite before answering. "I'm not sure."

"How about a dented old green car with a very loud engine that goes too fast? It nearly ran us over," Henry said.

Mr. Howe banged down his fork so hard the Aldens jumped. "Darn that Mr. Pitt! I told him and Mr. Lyme to slow down around here, especially at night. The speed limit's five miles an hour inside the motor court. I can't have them scaring my other guests!" With that, Mr. Howe forgot all about his pie and slid out from the booth. "I'm going over to their cabin right now and put a note on their door. They can find another place to stay in the morning!"

From the window, the Aldens watched Mr. Howe stomp down the road toward the cabins.

"Maybe we've seen the last of them and their old green car," Henry said before finally digging into his pie.

*   *   *

Benny and Violet were quiet the next morning as they hiked down Little Nose Cliff.

"I'm glad we're not going caving today," Violet said quietly. "Something always happens down there. I didn't like being lost yesterday."

"That's okay," Henry said. "We'll go rock hunting instead. Maybe today's the day we'll find a Rockville diamond."

Jessie read from Benny's rock book. "It says here to look for sections of rock that are different from the rest. Do you see anything like that, Henry?"

"Here and there," Henry answered. "Why don't I let Benny and Violet chisel away at those spots? We'll find a Rockville diamond yet."

But the Aldens had no luck. If there were any Rockville diamonds buried in the rock, they missed them. No matter how much the children hammered away, they didn't chip off anything but plain old rock.

Seeing Violet and Benny's disappointment,

Henry walked quite a few yards ahead to check farther down. As he was moving along the rock, he felt a cool breeze. Right away he knew what that meant. "Hey, another cave!" Henry yelled back to his brother and sisters. "We just have to move some of these loose rocks and dirt out of the way."

"It's a good thing I packed work gloves," Jessie said, when she and the others caught up with Henry. "It'll be easier to clear out the entrance so we can go inside."

With their hands, the Aldens scooped out a pile of rocks, stones, and dirt. When they were done, they found a foot-wide opening.

"That cool breeze from inside feels good," Jessie said, wiping her forehead with her bandana. "Look, there's plenty of room to get through if we go in sideways."

In the excitement of discovering a new cave, Violet and Benny soon forgot about getting lost the day before.

"Hey, neat!" Benny cried after he squeezed inside. "This is like a skinny doorway instead of a hole in the ground."

"I'm just going to tie this bandana to a

branch outside," Jessie said before joining the others. "Just in case. We won't go in too far since we don't have any of our caving equipment with us."

"Except for one flashlight," Henry said, patting his backpack.

The Aldens found themselves inside a large cave with a high ceiling and plenty of space to move around. Enough light came in from the entrance, so no one was too worried about getting lost.

"There's a passageway that goes off to the side," Henry said when he discovered a tunnel leading from the cave. "We'll come back another time when we have our tape and rope."

"I wonder if anybody else knows about this section of the caves," Jessie said, looking around. "I forgot to check for footprints before we covered up everything with our own footprints."

"Never mind footprints," Henry said, bending down to get a closer look at the cavern floor. "Look at these holes."

The other three children came over to see what Henry was talking about. When Jessie shone the flashlight on the ground, they saw one, two, three huge holes. Each one was surrounded by a mound of mud, small rocks, and dirt.

Suddenly, Jessie grabbed Henry's arm. "Did you say something?" she whispered. "I just heard a voice."

"I hear two voices," Violet whispered. "They're getting closer."

Henry pointed to the wall. "Move over there into that crawl space. I'll turn off my flashlight until we find out who's down here."

In the dark, the Aldens squeezed themselves into a tight space carved into the cave wall. The next thing they heard were footsteps squishing through the nearby tunnel.

"You and your stupid ideas," a man's angry voice said, just a few feet away. "Do you know how many tunnels are down here?"

The Aldens recognized the second voice they heard. It belonged to Randall Pitt. "Don't worry, Ed, we'll find it. He said it's down here. We just have to be patient."

"Patient? After you lost our other shovel

and then got us lost, too? What if somebody else finds it first?" Mr. Lyme shouted. "These caves are crawling with people."

"Nobody's looking for what we're looking for," Randall Pitt said. "So don't worry."

Before Ed Lyme could answer, Benny felt his nose tickle. He tried not to think about the tickle. "Go away, go away," he whispered to himself.

"What did you say, Benny?" Violet whispered.

"Ah — ah — ah-choo!" Benny cried when he couldn't hold his sneeze in any longer.

"What was that?" Mr. Lyme shouted just a few feet away from the Aldens. "Who's there?"

The children squeezed together as close as they could and prayed Benny wouldn't sneeze again.

"It can't be those snoopy kids. I figure they were scared off after we pulled up all their tape, cut the rope on the oldest one, and made up that story about a cave-in," one of the men said, shining his flashlight into the cavern.

Luckily for the Aldens, the men didn't see the crawl space the children were hiding in.

"Come on. Let's go down to the other end," Mr. Pitt said. "We already dug here and didn't find anything."

Then the men walked down the tunnel, dragging and scraping a shovel behind them. The Aldens waited several minutes before moving from their hiding space.

"Whew," Henry said, stepping out from the crawl space. "They're gone."

"So Mr. Pitt was the one who took down our tape," Violet said.

"That was Mr. Pitt all right. And you know who else that was?" Henry pointed his flashlight on the cave floor.

"Our monster!" Benny answered. "Their big wading boots made the footprints, and the shovel they were dragging made the tail prints."

"Good detective work!" Jessie said. "I hope you're not disappointed. You were hoping there was a monster."

"Disappointed? Not me," Benny said.

But he was — just a little.

CHAPTER 8

Violet Finds a Treasure

The Aldens wriggled out of the cave to have lunch in a warm, sunny spot.

"Let's put down our picnic blanket right here," Henry said. "That way we can keep an eye on this cave."

Jessie set out the sandwiches. "What is it about these caves?" she wanted to know. "Every time we go inside, somebody wants us out of there. First it was Crystal Hollowell. Now it's Mr. Pitt and Mr. Lyme."

"They're searching for something, that's for sure," Henry said. "But what could be

under all that mud and dirt?"

"Real diamonds!" Benny answered, very sure of that. "Those bad guys made big holes with that shovel. And know what? Maybe Joe Caveman is their partner, too. He had a book that said *Treasure* on it. Diamonds are treasure."

"Now don't get your hopes up," Violet said, looking up from Benny's rock guide. "Your book says nearly all diamonds are found in South Africa. I don't think diamonds are the treasure everyone's looking for in the caves."

Jessie borrowed the rock book. "I'm going to read about the Rockville diamonds again to see if we can't find our own treasure. Now where's that page with the — hey, wait! Look at the photographer's name under the picture of this rock."

Henry studied the photo Jessie was pointing to. "It says: 'photograph by Crystal Hollowell.' "

"Crystal Hollowell!" Jessie cried. "It can't be the same person. She said she studied animals."

Violet looked over Jessie's shoulder. "That's what she said, but when we saw her in the cave, she was doing something with rocks."

Jessie flipped through the pages of the rock book. "Listen! It says here that sometimes streaks of *silver* are found inside a special kind of lead. And, listen to this: 'Such lead deposits can be found in certain types of limestone.' These caves are made of limestone! I bet that's what Miss Hollowell and everybody else is looking for — silver!"

"I bet for sure that Miss Hollowell took this picture," Benny said. "Maybe if we don't find our Rockville diamonds, we'll find silver instead. Then we'll be rich."

Jessie laughed. "It's hard to find the kind of silver they're talking about in this book, Benny. You have to be a rock expert to know what to look for. Those men were searching for something, and so was Miss Hollowell. But maybe it's not silver, maybe it's something else."

"But what?" Violet asked.

"Don't forget Joe Caveman!" Benny cried.

"How can we forget Joe Caveman?" Jessie

said with a laugh. "You won't let us!"

"Can we go back into this cave?" Benny begged. "Can we?"

"I'd like to go back, too," Violet added, forgetting all her worries about getting lost.

Henry nodded. "Sure thing! I'm glad you changed your minds. I'd sure like to snoop around in there. But first let's go back to the cabin and get our safety gear. Oh, one other thing. We have to let Mr. Howe know we'll be caving here this afternoon."

After gathering up their things, the Aldens waited by the side of the road for the traffic to go by.

Suddenly, a truck that was driving by slowed down in front of the Aldens. But a second later, it sped up again and disappeared.

"Did you see who that was?" Henry asked.

"Crystal Hollowell," Jessie answered. "She took off like a rocket when she saw who we were."

Jessie checked down the road. "If we run, maybe we can see if she went to the other cave. It's not far from here."

"Good idea," Henry said. "Let's go."

Jessie was right. After racing down a ways, the Aldens spotted Crystal Hollowell's truck. Then they saw her, right by the sink-hole entrance.

"Let's try to catch up with her," Jessie said. "Oh, Miss Hollowell, Miss Hollowell!"

Hearing her name, Crystal Hollowell whirled around to see who was shouting for her. When she saw the Aldens, she marched back to her truck and threw her big duffel bag inside.

Jessie ran over to the truck. "Wait up. We wanted to ask you something. Benny, hand me your rock book."

By the time Benny pulled his book from his backpack, Crystal Hollowell had started up her truck. "I'm in a hurry, so step back."

But Jessie Alden was much too fast for Crystal Hollowell. She opened the rock book and stuck it through the truck window. "Did you take this photo, Miss Hollowell? It has your name underneath it."

"I have no idea what you're talking about!" Miss Hollowell answered without even looking at the book. "I've got to go." With that, the young woman stepped on the gas and sped away.

The Aldens hurried back to the cabin to get their safety gear.

When they came down from the Little Nose Cliff again, they had everything they needed to go caving — except time.

"I guess we should just look around the big cave we found this morning," Henry said. "There's not enough time to go back to the sinkhole cave, too. Besides, I left a note to Mr. Howe telling him where we'd be and that we marked the place with a bandana."

"The bandana!" Violet cried when the Aldens started searching for the cave entrance. "It's gone!"

The children walked along slowly, checking along the rock for the opening they had entered just hours before.

"This is strange. I don't see the entrance we dug out," Henry said. He ran his hand along the rock to feel for the cool spot. "It should be easy to find since we scooped out all that rock and dirt."

Benny ran ahead to look for the spot. "I'll find it! I'll find it!" But he found no bandana sticking out and no cave opening.

"A cave can't just disappear," Jessie said, walking up and down. "Let's think. This morning when we crossed the road, we were standing next to that road sign. The cave opening has to be right near there."

"Hey, the entrance has been covered up! That's why we didn't see it," Henry shouted when he checked the rock. "Somebody took the dirt and rock we dug out and pushed it back into the entrance!"

It didn't take long for the Aldens to dig out the entrance again. Soon, they were inside the cave. Now that they had four flashlights, there was plenty of light inside.

"Hey, there are those bootmarks again — the ones with the heels," Jessie said, aiming her flashlight at the cave floor. "Those aren't our footprints, and they're not big enough to belong to Mr. Pitt or Mr. Lyme. Let's follow them."

Henry cut up many pieces of reflective tape. "This time we'll put lots of tape high and low. Benny, take this stick and drag it along the floor as we walk. Whenever we get to a turn, make an 'X' in the mud. If we leave enough markers, there's no way anyone can erase every single one."

With their safety rules all set, the Aldens walked through the tunnel that branched off from the first room of the cave.

"Wow!" Benny yelled a few minutes later, running ahead. "You won't believe what I just found."

Benny's voice was coming from a room-sized space off the side of the tunnel. Squeezing in behind, Henry, Jessie, and Violet beamed their flashlights into the space.

"It's like a small living room," Violet said. "There's a folding stool, some books — even a sleeping bag."

"Whom could this belong to?" Jessie said.

"Not to the person we're trailing, that's for sure," Henry said, aiming his flashlight at the floor. "There's only one set of footprints in here, and they're way bigger than the ones we were following."

Violet picked up a book lying on the stool. "Look what I found."

The other children's eyes grew huge. Soon everyone was laughing very hard.

"It's — it's . . ." Henry started to say before he burst into laughter again.

"*Treasure Island*," Jessie finally managed to say between fits of laughter. "It's the book Joe Caveman was carrying the day we saw him. He wasn't looking for a treasure at all. He was just reading — "

"*Treasure Island!*" Benny cried. "That's the book you read me last summer about a shipwreck."

Jessie put her arm around Benny. "Remember how much you liked it?"

Benny nodded. "Not as much as I like real treasures. That's a funny joke on us."

The next thing the children heard wasn't a funny joke at all. Loud, stomping footsteps echoed in the cave.

"Quick!" Henry whispered. "Turn off

your flashlights. Maybe we can see who's going by."

"Or coming in," Violet whispered when a bright spotlight suddenly lit up the chamber.

"Who's in here?" a man's voice boomed.

There was no use hiding. The Aldens came out from the shadows.

"Joe Caveman!" the children yelled all at once.

"I guess you found my hideout," the tall stranger said.

Benny burst out with a question. "What are you hiding in your hideout?"

Joe Caveman pointed to himself. "Me. I'm hiding me."

Violet swallowed hard. "Is someone looking for you?"

For the first time, Joe Caveman smiled. "Everybody's looking for me, young lady. My five children, my wife, my boss. I never get a second to myself. I come down here for some peace and quiet on my days off to do a little reading and some exploring. I'm a spelunker."

"We're 'lunkers, too," Benny said. "But we

don't read books down here. We're looking for diamonds and silver and two men who made us get lost."

"Whoa, young fella, slow down," Joe Caveman said. "I hope you folks weren't the ones who hammered the walls at the sinkhole entrance where I first ran into you. There were some rock chips over there."

"That wasn't us," Benny said. "That was a lady who tried to scare us. She said we'd get flooded even though it was sunny out."

"Never saw her," Joe Caveman said. "As for the two men you mentioned, I wonder if they're the pair I chased out of here after I caught them digging up the cave."

"We saw them, too," Jessie said. "They took down all our reflective tape to scare us, and they cut our brother Henry's rope. Everybody seems to want us out of here."

Violet looked up at the tall stranger. "Do you want us out of here, too?"

Joe Caveman smiled at Violet. "Not at all. Sorry I was so gruff the other day. I'd just settled my things down in a good spot when those men came down making a racket with

their digging and yelling. All these caves connect, so I moved on and found this hideout
farther in. But caves are public places —
wonderful places if you know what you're
up to. I can see you children are very careful
cavers, so I don't mind that you're down
here. Hope I didn't scare you the other day."

"You did," Benny said with a laugh. "But
not for long."

"Good." Joe Caveman picked up his belongings. "I guess I'll be off. Half the fun is
trying to discover a spot where nobody can
find me."

With that, Joe Caveman was gone.

Benny ran after him. "Hey, wait!" he said.
"You forgot something."

Joe Caveman turned around. "What?"

Benny handed Joe Caveman his book.
"Your treasure."

CHAPTER 9

Trapped Underground!

After saying good-bye to Joe Caveman, the Aldens spent the rest of the afternoon exploring the new cave.

"Know what?" Benny asked as he walked along with his brother and sisters. "Joe Caveman never told us his real name."

"I like the name you gave him way better than any real name," Violet said. "Henry, why are you stopping?"

"Because we hit a dead end," Henry said when he came to a rock wall.

Jessie checked her watch. "It's four

o'clock. We should get back before Mr. Howe worries about us. And don't forget. Grandfather will be back tonight. We have to pack for Greenfield."

"Nuts!" Benny said when they turned back. "I didn't find a Rockville diamond or any silver or figure out any mysteries to tell Grandfather."

"We found out about Joe Caveman," Henry said. "That was a mystery we solved."

"That wasn't a *real* mystery. He was just a plain old person reading his book in a cave," Benny complained.

When the Aldens spotted the last piece of tape, Henry pulled it down. "Wait a minute. Is this where we started? I don't see the exit. There's no light in here except for our flashlights."

Jessie went over to the far wall of the cave. "The entrance is blocked!"

Henry came over and began to dig out rocks and dirt from the opening.

"What's the matter, Henry?" Violet asked.

Henry waited a long time before answering. "There's a boulder or something very heavy pushed against the outside. It's way too heavy for me to move."

"Are we trapped?" Benny asked, his voice cracking.

Jessie tried not to sound scared. "I've got an idea. Let's go back to where we saw Joe Caveman leave. He went out a different way. We'll just follow his footprints, and I know we'll get out."

The Aldens walked quickly back through the dark cave.

"Benny, you stick up the tape this time," Henry said. "And Violet can drag the stick along and mark our turns with an 'X.' Let's get a move on."

Finally, they were back in Joe Caveman's "living room."

"Okay," Jessie said, "here are Joe Caveman's footprints. Let's just follow them until we see daylight."

"Wait, I think I hear something," Henry said.

"Stop! I hear water rushing near here," said Jessie.

"Is it a flood, Jessie?" Benny asked. "What if there's a big thunderstorm outside?"

"Let's check where the sound is coming from," Jessie said as calmly as she could. "Maybe it's just an underground stream. That would be good because it could lead us out of here."

Everyone listened very carefully. Sure enough, there was a whooshing, gurgling sound nearby, so the Aldens headed in that direction.

"See, an underground stream!" Jessie whispered when they found water. "Let's walk along this ledge and see where it goes."

Henry led everyone alongside the stream. The Aldens hadn't gone far when they heard men's voices shouting in the distance.

"This is your dumbest idea ever," Ed Lyme said to Randall Pitt. "I'm not getting into that thing. I can't swim."

Mr. Pitt was blowing up a large raft with an air pump.

"Hey, what are you kids doing here?" Mr. Lyme shouted when he saw the Aldens standing there.

"It's us, Mr. Lyme," Henry explained. "Even though you tried to scare us, we decided to explore these caves anyway."

"What are you staring at?" Mr. Pitt asked when he noticed Henry staring at his head.

"So you're the one who broke into our cabin and stole my headlamp. I can see the initials I marked on it — H.A. And that's not all you stole. Nelly Stoner said a raft was taken from the Dragon's Mouth Cavern a couple of days ago."

Mr. Pitt kicked the raft to one side and took the headlamp off his head. "What are you talking about, kid?"

Mr. Lyme shifted from one foot to the other. "Come on, Randy. We need to talk. In private, without four pairs of ears listening in."

Then the two men moved several feet away so the Aldens wouldn't hear them.

Henry and Jessie didn't waste any time. "Come on," Jessie whispered to Benny and Violet. "Hop on the raft. First, let's put on these life jackets."

With barely a splash, the four children

climbed onto the raft. Henry pushed off with the oars and quickly began rowing.

The next thing the Aldens heard was a lot of yelling. "Hey! They took our raft!" Mr. Pitt screamed.

"Hey! They took our raft," the cave walls echoed back.

"Go after it!" Mr. Lyme shouted at Mr. Pitt.

But it was too late. The Aldens were soon floating along the current of a small stream.

CHAPTER 10

Back in the Dragon's Mouth

"Hey, I know where we are," Benny cried when the raft drifted into a huge, well-lit space. "We're in the Dragon's Mouth Cavern again!"

Henry rowed over to the wooden steps where the empty tour boat was tied up, and everyone got off the raft.

"I think we should call the police," Jessie said when they made their way to the elevator. "Those men took this raft and Henry's headlamp."

Henry pressed the elevator button, and the

children stepped inside. When the doors opened into the gift shop, everyone headed for the ticket booth where Mr. Alden was waiting.

"Grandfather!" Violet cried. "You're back."

"And you're back, children," Mrs. Stoner said, happy to see the Aldens. "I was getting worried about your being in the caves so late. Mr. Howe and I were almost about to go out looking for you since it was getting dark."

"You never would have found us," Benny said. "Never, ever. Somebody stole our tape markers so nobody could find us. Then the entrance was all stuffed with rocks and things. And a big rock, too! Even Henry couldn't push it out of the way."

"Whoa! Slow down, Benny," Grandfather said. "I see a thing or two happened while I was away."

"Can we call the police first?" Jessie asked Mrs. Stoner. "We found the people who took your raft. They're still in the caves. I think they were on your tour the other day."

After a quick call to meet the police near

the cave, everyone piled into Mr. Alden's
station wagon. Mrs. Stoner gave directions
while Benny brought Grandfather up to date
on all the excitement. When Mr. Alden
pulled up to the cave, a police car was already
there, parked next to Mr. Pitt's old green car.

"You folks seem to know these caves better
than we do," one of the two officers said.
"Can you lead the way down?"

"Just follow us," Henry said.

One by one the children slipped into the
cave entrance. The two officers followed
right behind.

"If we just go in a little, the cave branches
off in three directions," Jessie explained. "If
we wait there, the men have to come out one
of those tunnels if they plan to go back to
their car again."

The police and the Aldens didn't have to
wait long. They soon heard the sound of
heavy steps squishing through the muddy
cave.

"Stop!" one of the officers said when Mr.
Pitt and Mr. Lyme came into the tunnel.

"What is this all about?" Mr. Pitt demanded.

"It's about a stolen raft," the police officer began.

"And Henry's missing headlamp, too," Benny added.

Mr. Pitt tried to run in the other direction, but one of the police officers grabbed him first. "Stay where you are. You have some explaining to do, Randall Pitt."

"You know him?" Henry asked.

"Both of them," the officer answered. "They're a couple of petty criminals who can't stay out of trouble. They just finished six months' time in the county jail. I see they're up to their old tricks again."

Mr. Pitt's partner kicked at the ground. "I told you not to take that headlamp. A lot of good it did us. We never found the money, anyway."

"What money is he talking about?" the police officer asked Mr. Pitt.

"The money from the Rockville Union Bank robbery ten years ago," Mr. Pitt answered. "We overheard one of the robbers at the jail say he hid it down in these caves."

The two police officers started laughing and couldn't stop.

"What's so funny?" Benny asked.

One of the officers finally stopped laughing. "What's so funny is that the money they're talking about was fake — worthless. The bank gave the thieves counterfeit money. It was worth less than a pile of old newspapers! Now I'm going to put you two back where you came from — only this time for stealing a raft and a headlamp. That's pretty funny, too! But most of all, you should be ashamed of yourselves for trying to scare these kids."

Mr. Pitt and his partner weren't laughing a bit. Instead they argued with each other all the way out of the cave. When the police car pulled away, the Aldens could still hear the two men bickering in the back seat.

"That's a pretty good mystery you solved," Grandfather Alden said after his grandchildren explained about Mr. Pitt and Mr. Lyme.

"Finally," Benny said, giving Grandfather and Nelly Stoner a big smile. "But we can't leave Rockville until we solve another one. What was Miss Hollowell doing down in the caves?"

"And why didn't she want anyone else around?" Jessie asked.

Nelly Stoner smiled back. "I think that mystery is solved, too," she said. She handed Jessie a newspaper and pointed to a picture of Crystal Hollowell.

Jessie read what it said under the photo:

Rock expert Dr. Crystal Hollowell, a scientist from the Western College of Mines, has just reported a major discovery of silver inside local limestone caves. This is the first time this type of rock has been uncovered in this area.

"When I saw the picture, I figured out why her name seemed familiar," Nelly Stoner said. "She's a geologist who helped develop a new way to locate silver. I read about this in some of my journals, but I didn't make the connection to this young woman."

"I bet she was the one who blocked off the tunnel with the rock that said 'Keep Out,' " Violet said.

"And look, she's wearing heeled boots in the picture," Benny added, using his sharp eyes. "I bet the footprints near that rock belonged to her and her helper."

Nelly Stoner opened the newspaper and turned to one of the inside pages with a longer story. "This article says that she was afraid a rival would find the special rock. After she and her assistant blocked the tunnel inside the caves, they pushed one big rock outside another cave entrance so no one could get in."

"Or out," Henry said. "I guess she wasn't really trying to trap anybody on purpose — just keep them away."

"My, my," Mr. Alden said. "You must have had quite a fright being walled in. I'd like to take a look at the place."

A short ride later, the children led their

grandfather to the sinkhole cave by the side of the road. Mr. Howe was already there, helping a work crew fence in the entrance.

"Hello, Aldens," Mr. Howe said. "I suppose you heard that Crystal Hollowell discovered some valuable rocks on my property. With her new methods, she and some other rock experts — and I hope Nelly here — are going to go through and see if there's enough silver in these caves to go after. Meanwhile, it's off-limits to everyone but my guests."

"Does that mean us?" Benny wanted to know. "We want to show Grandfather how we got trapped inside this great big dark cave, but we weren't even scared."

Mr. Howe patted Benny's head. "Go right in, young fella. You just have to get some of those smaller rocks out of the way. Dr. Hollowell blocked up the entrance until she could get some other rock experts here."

Benny dug out some rocks from the opening and dropped them to the ground. "Ouch!" he said, when one of the rocks landed on his toe. He started to toss the heavy rock to the side when the sunlight hit it just right. At that moment, the rock sent out a rainbow of lights.

"Well, Benny," Jessie said, taking a closer look at the rock. "You discovered something, too."

"Miss Hollowell found a little bit of silver. But look what I found," Benny said, jumping up and down. "A real Rockville diamond!"

GERTRUDE CHANDLER WARNER discovered when she was teaching that many readers who like an exciting story could find no books that were both easy and fun to read. She decided to try to meet this need, and her first book, *The Boxcar Children*, quickly proved she had succeeded.

Miss Warner drew on her own experiences to write the mystery. As a child she spent hours watching trains go by on the tracks opposite her family home. She often dreamed about what it would be like to set up housekeeping in a caboose or freight car — the situation the Alden children find themselves in.

When Miss Warner received requests for more adventures involving Henry, Jessie, Violet, and Benny Alden, she began additional stories. In each, she chose a special setting and introduced unusual or eccentric characters who liked the unpredictable.

While the mystery element is central to each of Miss Warner's books, she never thought of them as strictly juvenile mysteries. She liked to stress the Aldens' independence and resourcefulness and their solid New England devotion to using up and making do. The Aldens go about most of their adventures with as little adult supervision as possible — something else that delights young readers.

Miss Warner lived in Putnam, Connecticut, until her death in 1979. During her lifetime, she received hundreds of letters from girls and boys telling her how much they liked her books.